Baby, I'm Yours

Caroline and Tom met on the Jersey Shore in the summer of 1965. Their attraction was instantaneous and strong, but the timing was wrong: Caroline was a young divorcee, trying to figure out a future that didn't include her cheating ex-husband, and Tom was about to deploy to Vietnam.

When he left her the morning after their passionate night together, Tom thought he'd never see Caroline again. But neither of them is ready to give up the connection they found with each other. Letters are the only way they can keep in touch, but what these two are sharing just might burn up the postal system. Can this sizzling correspondence sate their desire . . . for now?

In a heart-melting tale of love in the time of war, Caroline and Tom learn that trusting their hearts may be the most important battle they'll face.

This is a work of fiction. Similarities to real people, places, or events are entirely coincidental.

BABY, I'M YOURS
First edition. February 9, 2016.

Copyright © 2016 Emma Fallon
Written by Emma Fallon
Cover by Olivia Hardin

ISBN: 978-1-68230-401-3

All rights reserved. Without limiting the rights under copyright reserved above, no part of this publication may be reproduced, stored in or introduced into retrieval system, or transmitted, in any form, or by any means (electronic, mechanical, photocopying, recording, or otherwise) without the prior written permission of both the copyright owner and the above publisher of this book.

This is a work of fiction. Names, characters, places, brands, media, and incidents are either the products of the author's imagination or are used fictitiously. The author acknowledges the trademarked status and trademark owners of various products referenced in this work of fiction, which have been used without permission. The publication/use of these trademarks is not authorized, associated with, or sponsored by the trademark owners.

This book is licensed for your personal enjoyment only. This book may not be re-sold or given away to other people. If you would like to share this book with another person, please purchase an additional copy for each recipient. If you're reading this book and did not purchase it, or it was not purchased for your use only, then please return to your favorite book retailer and purchase your own copy. Thank you for respecting the hard work of this author.

Chapter One

Fort Dix, New Jersey

June 20, 1965
Dear Caroline,
I told myself I wasn't going to write back to you. What I said to you last night—this morning??—is still true. You need to find your life, and you're not going to be able to do that if you're sitting around waiting for me.

But I guess it turns out I'm selfish, because here I am. I'd like to say I'm writing this but maybe I won't send it. But hell. I know I will, because Caroline, you got to me. I wasn't even with you for twenty-four hours, but it's the truth. When I left you this morning, it felt like I'd torn out my insides and left them, too. It's crazy. How can I feel like that when we only met yesterday?

Okay, I'm going to stop asking questions now. I'm back in the barracks, and I have to say, it's pretty depressing. Everyone knows we're close to deploying, and the guys who're leaving their wives and girlfriends are the quietest of all. I guess I'm part of that crew now. Not that you're my girlfriend. I didn't ask you to be, and I don't expect anything from you. But I'd be lying if I said you're not something to me. So that's it, you're my something.

I'm pretty sure you said you were staying down at the shore for another week or so. That means you won't get this until you go back to your parents' house. I hope everything's okay there. I get the feeling you're unhappy to still be living with them. Tell me what you're planning to do, how you're going to take back your life. Because I know you will.

The guy whose bunk is above mine got married right before he came here. He's from Tennessee, and so he didn't have enough time to go see her when we had leave. But I guess she found out and managed to get here to surprise him at the last minute. He told me they only had two hours together before he had to report back, but he wouldn't have given up those two hours for anything. I guess I know how he feels, because even though we only had about twelve hours, I'm pretty sure it was the best half day of my entire life.

And not just because of the sex, although— damn, baby, the sex was out of sight. But even if we'd just had dinner and talked, you'd still be on my mind. There's just something about you, and when I think of your eyes laughing up at me. Or the way your hair spread out on the pillow when you were laying beneath me. Damn, I need to stop thinking about you or sleeping's never going to happen.

I got to hit the hay, babe. PE starts at 0500 and that comes early. But when you get this, know I'll be dreaming of you.

Tom

June 23, 1965
Dear Caroline,
I wasn't going to write again before I knew you were back at home with your parents. I wanted to give you a chance to decide if you wanted to write me back. But it turns out I'm not going to be here much longer, so I figured I'd send one more before I might not be able to do it for a while.

Everything is gearing up in our unit, and it's like we have this whole different energy. The guys are both tense and excited. A lot of the younger ones are all gung-ho to get over there and kick some commie ass—that's what they say. The older guys who've been there already are a lot quieter.

And me—I don't know. I signed up for this because I wanted to get out of town. You remember that, right? I enlisted because I thought I was in love with Molly, my best friend's girl. His fiancée. When I told her how I felt, she told me I needed to get out of town after their wedding. I didn't tell you this, but the day I left, Molly said she thought I'd just move to San Francisco or something. She didn't mean I had to go half way around the world. I remember thinking, 'yeah, but that's how far I have to go to forget you.'

But ironically, turns out I only had to go to the Jersey shore on the right day to find the person who'd make me forget Molly.

So now I'm feeling like a fool, signing up to get shot at in Southeast Asia just because I thought I had a crush on my friend's girl. What an idiot. And then I started thinking last night while I was trying to get to sleep . . . if I hadn't been that idiot and enlisted, I wouldn't have been in New Jersey at all this summer. Probably I'd have been working in Pasadena, living the same old life. I never would've met you. And crazy as it might sound, meeting you is more than a fair trade off for eighteen months of army life.

Okay, gotta go. Things are getting fast and furious right now, getting us set to go. I can't say when we're leaving, but by the time you get this, I won't be in the state anymore.

I've put my new address at the top of this letter. But Caroline, if you get home from the shore and realize you don't want to answer this, don't. I'll understand, and I'll trust that if it's meant to be, we'll run into each other some other time, some other place.

Tom

Chapter Two

Woodville, New Jersey

I stood in the middle of my bedroom, staring down at the two envelopes in my hand. They were thin white paper, and the handwriting in black ink on the front was unfamiliar, and yet—somehow not.

He wrote to me. He really wrote to me.

I'd been back from Ocean City for about thirty minutes. My mother had greeted me at the door, asked about my drive up out of force of habit—it was what we did, after all. If someone had been down the shore, we always asked about the traffic. I'd assured my mother that my ride home had been uneventful, and then I'd turned toward the hallway, heading to my bedroom so I could dump my suitcase and get cleaned up. I'd come right from the beach, not wanting to waste a single minute in the sunshine.

"Oh, these came for you." She was trying to keep her voice casual, nonchalant, but failing miserably. I glanced over my shoulder, and my heart jumped into my throat when I spied the two envelopes in her hand.

"Thanks." I managed to stop and reach for the letters without shaking, which was pretty amazing.

"They're postmarked Fort Dix." My mother added that helpful bit of information.

"Uh huh." I started walking again.

"Who do you know in Fort Dix?" She'd given in and was finally asking me a direct question.

"Oh, you know. You meet people." There was no way in hell I was telling her anything about Tom. He was mine for now, a memory I'd been hugging to my heart for the last twelve days. And if I'd told her the truth, she'd probably drop dead of a coronary right here.

Oh, Mom, these are from Tom. I met him at the beach right after I got to Ocean City, and I let him drive my car and take me to dinner, and then I invited him to spend the night at Aunt Susan's house. With me. Just the two of us. Alone. And while he was there, he fucked my brains out and taught me more about my body and sex and making love than anyone else has in all my life.

She'd have been unconscious by the word *fuck*.

Instead, I kept my mouth shut even as she'd followed me into my room. I didn't miss the frown of concern, the little wrinkle between her eyebrows. In an effort to throw her off the scent, I tossed the letters onto my bed, as if they meant nothing to me.

"But Caroline—"

Her tone told me that if I engaged, I'd end up either lying to her or coming clean about my Ocean City tryst. Neither option was one I liked. So I dropped my bag onto the floor of my bedroom and shot her a bright smile.

"I'm going to take a shower, and then maybe we can have some lemonade and you can tell me all about the wedding."

My suggestion had its intended result. "Oh, yes! Wait'll I tell you what Uncle Walt did at the reception." She patted my arm. "You clean up, and I'll wait for you in the kitchen."

I waited until her heels clicked down the hall before I closed the door, sagging against it. My heart was pounding, but I didn't immediately leap for the envelopes. Instead, I stared at them for a few minutes, just savoring the sight of the one thing I'd been afraid to hope for over the past days.

He'd written to me.

I took a step closer to the bed and picked up the letters. Without thinking about it, I lifted the paper to my nose and sniffed, hoping to catch a whiff of that elusive scent that was only Tom's . . . but of course, it only smelled like paper and ink. And maybe a little like my mother's lemon polish, probably because they'd been sitting on the front table since they'd arrived.

Examining the postmarks, I saw that one of the letters had been sent right after Tom had been with me in Ocean City, and the other a few days later. I slid my finger beneath the flap of the first one, pulling out two sheets of paper as I crawled onto the bed and leaned against the pillows.

Warm gladness spread through me as I read the lines. *When I left you this morning, it felt like I'd torn out my insides and left them, too.* That was how I'd felt, too, when he walked out of the beach house. It was as though he'd ripped out my heart and carried it with him through the door. I hadn't left the house for the rest of that day; instead, I'd alternated between sleeping fitfully and crying.

I smiled when I came to the part where he'd decided I was his *something.* His something. Well, something was better than nothing, and I remembered what he'd told me that magical night. He'd said that if he hadn't been about to leave for Vietnam, he'd drag me down to the courthouse and marry me. I knew he'd meant it.

My thumb rubbed against the third finger of my left hand, at the spot where a ring had been for two years. I was just getting used to being without that ring, but right now, I wished Tom's ring had replaced the emptiness. If we'd been crazy and impetuous, I could be Tom's wife instead of just his something.

But that hadn't been possible. Tom had had to get back to post, and on some level, I'd known he was right when he said he had to leave me. Diving into a marriage before we'd even known each other a full day was insanity. After my experience with wedded bliss—which was pretty non-blissful—I had to be more careful than that. On the other hand, I'd known my jerk of an ex-husband for five years before we'd gotten married, and look how that had turned out.

I finished the first letter, read it through a second time, and then tucked it back into the envelope before I picked up the second. Turning it over in my hands, I debated whether I should read it now—gobble it up like a box of chocolates—or save it for later. Maybe for tonight, before bed. Give myself something to look forward to. That seemed prudent.

But of course, I was ripping it open before that thought had even completely formed in my head, grinning like a fool. My smile faded by the time I reached the end of the first paragraph.

He was leaving. He'd written again because they were deploying, shipping off to Vietnam. I skimmed over the next lines, pausing only when I came to a part near the end:

And crazy as it might sound, meeting you is more than a fair trade off for eighteen months of army life.

It was such a Tom thing to say. I could almost hear his voice, husky with want, and see his eyes, dark with desire. And suddenly I felt his leaving even more keenly.

In some part of my heart, I'd made myself a deal. If I made it through the two weeks at the shore and came home to a letter from Tom, driving up to Fort Dix would've been a fitting reward for my patience. It had never occurred to me that he'd be gone before I could make that happen. I knew he'd mentioned that his overnight leave was because of their imminent departure, but everyone knew how slow the Army moved. I'd figured imminent meant at least a month.

All this time that I'd been getting through the days, thinking Tom was in the same state with me, he'd been getting ready to leave and then flying away. I wondered if they were already in Asia. I didn't have any way of knowing, but since he'd told me to use the new address, it seemed like a pretty good bet.

And suddenly, I felt very alone once again.

~

I got through the rest of the day on auto-pilot. After I finished reading the second letter, I slid both of them into a book and then pushed that into the bookshelf. I wouldn't have put it past my mother to go snooping while I showered, and it would've killed me to have her read the words meant only for my eyes.

I showered, dressed and joined my mom in the kitchen. If she was still curious about the letters, she didn't show it; instead, she launched into a long and detailed description of my cousin's wedding, what each family member had worn, how the bride and groom had behaved and which uncles had gotten drunk. I listened, nodding and making the appropriate noises at the right times.

My father came home from work just before dinner, greeting me with his typical half-hearted kiss on the cheek. Ever since my divorce, I'd been something of an enigma to him. Up until then, I'd done the dutiful daughter deal to a T: high school, college, good grades, nice boys, engagement and wedding. He knew how to speak to me then, and he could tell his friends and co-workers about his son-in-law.

But once I broke the mold and divorced—even though it was James who both caused and initiated our split—Dad didn't know what to say to me. Mostly, he nodded at me in the morning and again at night. If I asked him a question, he'd reply. When he and my mother were chatting and I joined in, he didn't ignore me. But he never tried to start a conversation with me. It made me a little sad that I'd somehow let him down, even though none of it had been my fault. After my time with Tom, I was more sure of that than ever.

Mother fussed about dinner, jumping up to slide the meatloaf into the oven and make Dad his nightly cocktail. I tried not to think about the two letters sitting in my bedroom, waiting for me to respond, but all I want to do was run back there and read them again.

I got up to set the table, working around my father and his open newspaper. "I caught a couple of the Phils' games while I was down the shore, Daddy. Richie Allen's looking good."

"Hmm." He didn't look up from his paper. "Damn inconsistent is what they are."

"Well, they took all but one game in Houston and then split in San Francisco." In my childhood, baseball—particularly the Phillies—had been a passion my father and I had shared. I still loved to go over to Connie Mack to watch our boys of summer play, and I tried to use it as a way to communicate with my dad, but he had relegated me to the ranks of womanhood—and in his mind, that group was off-limits when it came to sports.

"Huh." He glanced at my mother. "How's that meatloaf coming along? I'm famished."

I swallowed back a sigh and helped my mother finish the potatoes. She didn't meet my eyes as we worked side-by-side until all the food was in bowls and on the table.

Dinner was business as usual with my parents. My mother kept up a steady patter of talk, my father put in a word here or there, as required, and I stayed silent, unless something was specifically addressed to me.

"Oh, Diana and Eddie will be home Friday, so I thought we might have a little family cook-out that night. What do you think, Hal? Wouldn't that be fun?"

I swallowed a bite of green beans. "Where were they?"

"Oh, you remember, Caroline." My mother shook her finger at me as though it might jog my memory. "They went up to the Poconos after the wedding."

I nodded. My sister and brother-in-law had been included in my cousin's wedding, whereas I, the family divorcee, was sent to my aunt's beach house so as not to embarrass anyone. Though I wouldn't have said it to my parents, I frankly thought I got the better end of the deal.

"Why do we need to make a fuss?" My dad spoke up. "It's not like we don't see them all the time anyway. They've just been gone a week."

"Because it's nice to celebrate once in a while." Mother's mouth tightened. "We should take advantage of it. DeeDee and Eddie and Caroline will all be home after being away."

Dad shrugged. "Do as you want. As long as I don't have to do anything. Ball game'll be on, and I just want to watch it and drink my beer."

What else is new . . . I bit my tongue to keep from saying the words and pushed my chair away from the table. "Mother, let me help you with the dishes."

Both of my parents stared up at me, surprised. "We're not finished eating yet."

I rubbed my forehead. "I'm sorry. I'm just so tired. You know how the beach takes it out of me . . . and then driving home . . ." I let my voice trail off.

"Oh, honey, you go rest. You helped with dinner. I can handle the dishes. Go on now, get some sleep. We'll see you in the morning."

"Are you sure?" Tom's letters were pulling me back toward my room like a siren call. I faked a big yawn.

"Of course. Shoo now."

I didn't wait for her to tell me again. Stopping only to brush a kiss over her cheek, I fled down the hall into the sanctuary of my bedroom.

Locking the door behind me—I didn't think my mother would bother me, but I had to be sure—I retrieved the letters and curled up on my bed to re-read them.

And then I pulled out the pink box that held all my stationary and my favorite pen.

June 30, 1965
Dear Tom,

I got home today from my two weeks at the shore. To be honest with you—and I promise, even if I think it's something you don't want to hear or something I don't want to tell you, I will always be honest with you—I wanted to leave the same day you did. Every part of me wanted to pack up and drive home, just to wait and see if you wrote to me.

But I didn't do it, for two reasons. One was something you said, that you didn't want me waiting by the mailbox for your letters—which you said you wouldn't write. I knew you didn't want me to do that. And the second reason I stayed was fear. I was terrified that you wouldn't write. And so those two weeks gave me the ability to live in a world where it was still possible that you would. I guess I'm just a coward.

So when I got here and my mother handed me your letters, it was like the sun came out again after a long stretch of gray. I gobbled up your first one, and then I read the second, and my heart plunged.

You're gone.

All this time, I'd been picturing you back at Fort Dix. I never thought you might leave before I even got home, although if you hadn't, I might've read your letter and driven up there to see you, whether you wanted me or not.

So here we are. Now that I've boo-hooed about myself, I'll just say please stay safe. Please write me when you can, even if it's just a line. I promise I won't sit around waiting to hear from you, but still.

I want to talk about your first letter to me. I was so happy—giddy—that you said that I'd gotten to you, because Tom, I haven't been able to stop thinking about you since that night. I told myself it's just because I've been so lonely. Because you were so kind to me. Because you are such a gorgeous hunk. But I know it's more, and I was relieved when you said you'd been thinking about me, too.

Probably shouldn't tell you this, but I stayed in bed all day after you left and just brooded. I railed at the fates, as my English teacher used to say. I wished with all my heart that I'd met you when I was seventeen, before I knew James and made the most massive mistake of my life. Can you imagine if we'd met then? Would we have gotten to know each other the same way we did over that short time together? I don't know. Those hours we had together felt special. Somehow magical.

You wrote in your second letter that if you hadn't fallen in love with Molly and then enlisted, we never would've met each other. But I wonder. You're originally from New Jersey, right? Maybe you would've come back . . . or if you'd never moved to California to begin with, we might've crossed paths in high school.

I guess that's stupid, huh? Talking about all these might've beens. I need to face reality and realize that the here and now is what's important, even though the now means that I'm here and you're . . . I guess you're somewhere in Vietnam.

You asked me to tell you what I'm going to do to take back my life. I thought about that, too, after you left. I imagined what might happen when you come back from Asia—I wouldn't want you to find me still living here with my parents, just killing time. So I have a plan. I'm going to move out and find a job. Or maybe find a job and move out. Either way, I'm taking control of my life again.

I'm going to write you again tomorrow, and probably the next day, too. My friends would all say I should wait to hear from you again, because maybe once you get some space and distance, you won't want to write back. But I don't care. I don't believe that.

If you do get my letter and decide not to write back, don't. Don't send me some lame excuse about what happened between us being just a fluke or something like that. Let me have my memories of that night. Because it changed my life, and because of what you taught me, I'm going to be a different person. I already am.

I'm going to bed now, and to repeat what you said . . . know I'll be dreaming of you, because I have every night for the last ten days.

P.S. I don't have a problem with you thinking of me as your girlfriend, but just in case you'd be uncomfortable calling me that, I'll just sign myself—
Caroline
Your Something

Chapter Three

July 26, 1965
Dear Caroline,
Or should I say my something?
I think I know a little bit of how you felt when you saw my letters, because even though I knew on some level that you weren't at home to get mine, some small part of me kept hoping to see your name on an envelope at every mail call. When I finally did, damn. I thought I was playing it cool, but my buddy Benny called me out. He said, "So the chick finally wrote back?" I asked him why he said that, and he said, "That's the biggest smile I've seen on your face since I knew you."

We're in country now, as they say. I've done some traveling in my time, because Aunt Cissy took me to Europe and to South America, but this is like no place I've ever been. The land—it's beautiful. We flew over the rice paddies coming in, and the colors and landscape are like something out of a dream. My unit's in a city right now, and that's not so pretty, at least not all the time. I thought since I'd been to San Francisco so much, I wouldn't find things so foreign, but it's not the same at all. Not bad, but not America.

Our days here are pretty routine right now. I'm with a Military Police unit, did I ever tell you that? So we patrol and we deal with stuff like black market sales and drugs—and keeping our boys safe and on the straight and narrow. Not an easy thing.

And you got to keep your head about you all the time. There're these street cafés, places that look like any place else, but you got to watch, because some of them aren't that safe. We've had bombings in those. I guess mostly what spooks me is that if you don't stay alert, you could fool yourself into thinking everything here is okay. But it's not, and sometimes the kid who asks you for a chocolate bar just might be the next one to throw a grenade.

But that's enough of that. I don't want you to worry, because honestly—and like you said, I'll always be honest with you—I'm not on the front lines. Not yet, anyway. I've heard buzz that they're sending more MP divisions over, and then we might be moved, but who knows? There's more rumors around here than anything else.

I like the guys in my unit. They're all cool. Benny's probably the one I feel most comfortable with, because he's got common-sense. Some of the other guys want to run around and do crazy things, and Benny and I are the ones rolling our eyes. He's married, and you can tell he worships the ground his wife walks on. They haven't been married that long, but they were childhood sweethearts. Both of them from the same small town in Tennessee. He was pretty disappointed the other night, because I guess she wanted a baby, and they were hoping she might be pregnant, and he just got a letter where she told him she isn't. I'm not sure if he's really sad about it or if he's just upset for her, but anyway . . . it made me think of us and our night. How I told you under other circumstances, I'd wouldn't worry so much about getting you pregnant. I wasn't kidding, but I'm glad I don't have to worry about that. I'd be going crazy over here, thinking about you doing that all by yourself.

When I thought about that, I started letting myself remember other stuff from that night. There's not much in the way of privacy around here, baby, but by last night, I didn't care. I waited until I was pretty sure everyone was asleep, and then I reached down, under the blanket, and I touched my cock. God, baby. It's been over a month since I left you in Ocean City, and still, just thinking about you in that bed makes me hard.

First I remembered touching your tits. You've got the most amazing nipples, you know . . .when I put my mouth on them, you arched so close to me, like you wanted me to take even more of you between my lips. They went stiff, and your hips moved like you were searching for me. Like your pussy wanted my cock. That got me thinking about the first time I touched you there, between your perfect legs. You were wet, slippery, and the feel of you on my fingers—I thought I might explode the minute my fingers made contact. And then you did. When you came the first time, it was honest-to-God the most beautiful thing I ever saw.

I kept rubbing my hand up and down my dick, remembering. I pictured my fingers sliding into you, and the way your pussy squeezed them when you came. Just thinking about that pushed me over the edge, and I came all over. I almost bit through my lip, trying to keep quiet so I didn't shout so loud I'd have woken up the entire barracks. I'd never hear the end of that.

I hope you've been touching yourself. You need to keep finding out what makes you feel good. What drives you wild. I know I told you to find a man who would be good to you, who'd let you keep learning more about your body. And Caroline, if you do, it's okay. If you meet a guy who gives you that spark, don't hesitate on my account. Don't give up something because you feel some kind of obligation to me. I'm going to be here at least eighteen months. That's a long fucking time, baby. If your life comes knocking, you answer that door. Promise me.

This turned out to be a lot longer than I meant it. But I had so much to get out, I guess. I can't wait to get your next letter and hear how everything's going with getting your life back on track.

And Caroline, baby . . . if you could send me a picture of yourself, I'd sure love that. Not that I've forgotten what you look like, but I think Benny's starting to think I made you up. I haven't said too much, but I told him I met a girl on our last leave, and I really liked her. I want him to see how beautiful you are, so he doesn't think he's the only one around here with a gorgeous woman in his life.

Until next time.
Tom

"Dee, can I ask you something?" I shifted in my lounge chair and shaded my eyes with one hand so I could see my sister better.

"Mmmmm." She turned her head a little and squinted at me. "What's up, Caro?"

"When you and Eddie . . . when you got married, was everything—good right away? I mean . . ." I was sure my face was bright red and that it had nothing to do with the heat. "In the bedroom."

"Caroline! For heaven's sake. What's wrong with you, asking something like that?" Diana pushed herself to sit up straighter, not looking at me. "God. Sometimes I think Mother dropped you on your head when you were a baby."

"I'm not asking for you to give me details. I just mean—" I sighed. "James said, when he left me, that I wasn't—that I didn't know what I was doing. In bed. He said I bored him, and that's why he did what he did."

"That's ridiculous." Dee's voice was harsh. She'd never liked my ex-husband, not before we'd married or after. Turned out my sister was an excellent judge of character.

"But I didn't know. It's not like you or Mother told me what to do, or what to expect. James seemed to think I should know."

Diana snorted. "Oh, really? So you were supposed to be completely innocent and completely experienced at the same time?"

"I don't know. I guess so." I shrugged. "I always thought that both of us were, uh, innocent. He never made me think otherwise."

"Men." She flipped her large black-framed sunglasses up on top of her head, pinched the bridge of her nose and then slipped the glasses back in place. "You know, Caroline, this divorce—it doesn't have to mean your life is over. I'm sure there are still plenty of men who might be interested in you."

An image of Tom with his head between my legs popped into my mind, and my cheeks went hot again.

"I mean, maybe a widower. An older man, someone who's not looking for—you know, fresh and young."

"Because I'm stale and old? Thanks, Dee. I can always count on you to lift my mood. So nice to know being someone's second best is the only thing I have to look forward to."

"Hey, beats living here for the rest of your life, right?" Dee pointed back at our parents' house. "I love them, you know, but it'd drive me insane to have to move back in. I can't believe you've lasted this long."

I curled my legs up and tucked my feet beneath me. "Well, I'm not lasting much longer. I'm moving out."

"What?" She turned to face me so fast that she nearly fell out of the chaise lounge. "What do you mean? Where're you going?"

I smiled. "I found an apartment last week and signed the rental agreement. I'm moving in ten days."

"Oh, my God." Dee's mouth fell open. "What did Mother and Dad say when you told them?"

"I haven't yet. I planned to do it tonight."

She smirked. "I'd tell you to call me after you break the news, but I have a feeling I'll hear Dad roar all the way from my house."

Butterflies flutter in my stomach, but I only shook my head. "Doesn't matter. He can roar all he likes, but I have my own money. It's time I have my own life, too. I'm done worrying about what Mother and Dad think. Actually, I'm done worrying about what anyone thinks."

"Whoa there. What happened to you down the shore? You must've come home a new woman."

I lifted one shoulder. "I had a lot of time to think. Plus, I found out I actually like being on my own. There's a brand-new high rise in Cherry Hill, and they had a one-bedroom available."

"And you can swing that? On just your—the money James is giving you?"

I rolled my eyes. "Dee, it's called alimony. It's not a dirty word. And yeah, I could do that, but it'd be tight. I'm going to look for a job once I get moved in."

My sister, having gotten over her shock, settled back into the chair. "Any idea what you're going to do?"

"Not really." I'd been checking out the classified ads as surreptitiously as I could, but my college degree was the all-too-vague liberal arts. I'd been engaged to James in our junior year of college, so the only future I'd planned was one as a wife and eventually a mother. "I guess maybe office work. I can type and I can answer phones."

"That sounds incredibly boring. Hey, do you want me to ask Eddie to check around in his building? Maybe someone has an opening."

"Sure, I guess. But nothing at his office, okay? I don't want to feel like I'm depending on charity."

"All right. I think you're being silly about that, but I'll tell him to keep it to the other businesses."

"Thanks."

We both laid our heads back and were quiet for a few minutes. I was just about to doze off when Diana spoke again.

"Caroline? What you asked before . . . about the bedroom." She cleared her throat. "Eddie slept with someone else before we got married. Before we got engaged, even."

I made a noise of surprise but let her go on.

"Remember when we broke up for that month? About a year and a half before we got married?"

"Of course I do. You moped around the whole time, listening to the most depressing jazz I'd ever heard."

Dee laughed. "I did, didn't I? Well, I found out later that he'd, uh, dated another girl during that time. So when we got married, I knew Eddie was more experienced than I was. But he was kind about it, Caro. He was patient and so sweet. Things haven't always been perfect between us, but we're good."

I was strangely grateful for my brother-in-law, whom I'd always seen as a stodgy guy. I was glad he was such a great husband to my sister. "That's wonderful, Dee. I'm happy for you."

She reached across the small space between our chairs and grabbed my hand, squeezing it. "The right person's going to come along for you, Caroline. Just you wait and see. And you'll be able to forget all about that dweeb James."

I didn't reply, but I thought about Tom. I was fairly certain I had met the right person, but he just happened to be thousands of miles away, in a foreign country where war and violence were the order of the day.

July 28, 1965
Dear Tom,
I was so happy to hear from you. I got four letters all in one day, so it felt like a jackpot, after waiting so long! I understand the mail's a little iffy there. It's okay. I can be patient.

Vietnam sounds both beautiful and terrifying. I can't imagine never knowing if stopping for a drink in a little café could end in an explosion. Please be careful.

First, before I say anything else, I have news: last week, I moved into my own apartment. This was a huge step for me. When I told my parents, my father said no. I knew he wasn't going to like it, but he actually tried to forbid me from doing it. And when I said I was going to move anyway, he said not to come crying to him when I wanted to move home in a month. Which made me vow to myself that no matter what happens, I'll never move back there again.

My dad refused to help me move, but my sister Diana, her husband Eddie and my mother all did help, which was good, because I had a lot of things that needed to be carried. I've been having a blast the last few days, setting up all the furniture and decorating. My sister laughs at me, because she says I'm more excited now than I was when James and I moved into our house. She's right. That never felt like mine, but this apartment does.

I was afraid that I might feel a little lonely and scared at night, but it hasn't happened yet. I turn on the hi-fi and play the radio or my records, and I read. I've been cooking, too. I forgot how much I like to do that. James was so picky about what he ate, and since I moved home, my mother never let me do anything in her kitchen other than help. I've been clipping recipes from magazines and trying new dishes.

And when I go to bed at night—I think of you. I must've re-read the letter where you wrote about touching yourself a hundred times. I'll admit, when I think about our night together, it makes me ache, wishing for you. As for making myself feel good? I haven't yet. I rubbed my fingers over my nipples a few times, because that didn't feel totally weird. But anything else? When I was a little girl and my hand would stray between my legs, my mother would say, "Caroline, don't do that. It's nasty." I guess I'm a chicken. And I'm not sure it would feel the same as when you were the one making me come alive.

But I think, and I remember. For instance, I remember what it felt like when I put my mouth on your cock. I never in a million years thought I'd do something like that. I didn't even know people did. It made me feel wild and adventurous and maybe even a little like a bad girl. Is that weird? I never thought of myself that way. I was the one who didn't go all the way, who dressed like a lady. Being a little bit wicked, just with you, felt really good.

Well, I guess I made this long enough. I added my new address to the bottom of this page, but don't worry if you sent a few letters to my parents' house. I'll be going back to pick up my mail. My mother raises her eyebrows at me every time she hands me one of your envelopes, but I ignore it and she hasn't said anything yet.

Tomorrow I'm going on a job interview. Hopefully, by the time you get this, I'll be gainfully employed. How's that for turning my life around?

And since you didn't ever answer my comment about being willing to be your girlfriend, I'll just keep calling myself—
Caroline

Your Something
P.S. What did you think of the picture I put in my last letter? I hope it was okay.

Chapter Four

"Dr. Newton will see you now."

I stood up and smoothed my dress over my legs, drawing in a deep breath to calm my nerves. Eddie had arranged this interview for a receptionist job through a friend of an associate. It had turned out that no one in his building was hiring, but someone he'd spoken to had a dentist friend looking for a receptionist.

Trying to ignore the nauseating smell all dental offices seemed to have, I followed the hygienist down a hall into a large office. She ushered me inside and pointed to a chair.

"Have a seat. The doctor will be with you shortly."

I perched on the edge of the hard chair, crossed my ankles and tucked them beneath me. My stomach churned; I'd never had a job interview before in my life. The closest I'd come was when I'd applied for the student body council back in college.

The door flew open behind me, and a man of medium height with short blond hair strode into the room. He glanced at me, looked away and then did a double-take, his eyes making a slow and sleazy trip down my body. Suddenly, I wanted to cross my arms over my boobs.

"Miss . . . Rogers, is it?" He moved around to sit on the opposite side of the desk and sat down.

"Caroline. Yes." I forced a smile that I hoped looked genuine. "Thanks for seeing me, Dr. Newton."

"Not at all. So you're interested in being our receptionist?"

Honestly, I wasn't. I couldn't think of anything more boring. But I needed a job, and this was one that had come my way.

"Yes, I am." My hands tightened on the small clutch purse in my lap. "I don't really have much experience—"

"Oh, really?" He raised one eyebrow, and his mouth twisted into a smirk.

"—in office work." I finished, working to keep my voice even. "But I'm a fast learner."

"Oh, I just bet you are." Dr. Newton leaned forward, his hands folded loosely on the desk blotter. "Tell me . . . Caroline. How on earth is a girl like you still single?"

My back stiffened. "Oh, it's a fun story. I met a boy in college, got married right after graduation, lived happily-ever-after for about two years before my loving husband decided he liked his secretary more than me. That means I'm not really single. I'm divorced."

I waited for him to react, but the good doctor only grinned bigger. "I've heard divorced girls are a lot of fun."

There wasn't any good way to answer that, so I tried re-direction. "What would this job entail, exactly? I assume I'd need to learn the telephone system, and maybe some filing?"

He waved his hand. "Oh, we'd get you up to speed, no problem. I'm not worried about that. I mean, a monkey can do that kind work." He winked. "That's why it's perfect for a pretty girl like you."

I gritted my teeth. This wasn't the first time I'd been treated as though my looks made my brain an also-ran. "If a monkey can do this work, maybe that's who you should hire. I don't need to use my pretty face or my body to get a job. I've got a college diploma."

Dr. Newton laughed. "Yeah, in what? Sending girls to college is a waste of time and money, unless they leave school with their MRS degree." He rose to his feet and circled the desk, getting closer to me. "And you, honey, couldn't hold onto that degree. But I know about girls like you. And I think we could have some fun if you came to work for me."

"That'd be just peachy." I stood up, too, putting the chair between him and me. "If I was interested in fun. But I'm not. I want a job, not just a front for getting groped by some jerk. So thanks, but no thanks."

Dr. Newton reached for me, and I didn't move my arm fast enough to get away. "Aw, honey, don't be so fast to make up your mind." His fingers dug into my upper arm as he tugged me closer. With his free hand, he cupped my breast, squeezing over the fabric of my dress. "I promise, I can give you a good time."

No man had touched me in that way—intimately—since Tom had left me in Ocean City almost two months before. Maybe before I might've been afraid, but today, remembering what Tom had told me—that I deserved to be with someone who treated me well, that sex was meant to be enjoyable, even fun, not something to get through—there was no way in hell I was going to let this jerk use me to get his jollies.

Instinct took over, and I raised my knee, ramming it into his balls. With a howl, Dr. Newton released my arm and doubled over, cursing me loudly.

"You fucking tease bitch, what the hell's the matter with you? Get out of here, you fucking bitch."

"Gladly. I wouldn't take a job from you if you were the last man hiring." I flung open the door and half-ran down the hall. The hygienist glanced up at me in alarm as I passed her.

"Your boss is a sexist pig. I hope you know that. Also, if I were you, I wouldn't be alone with him."

I slammed the door and bypassed the elevator, running down the steps instead. I felt dirty, as though the whole scene upstairs had been somehow my fault. My hands were shaking as I yanked open the door of the office building and stumbled into the sunlight.

For a few minutes, I simply stood there, not sure what to do next. I didn't have any other interviews set up. My Mustang was parked down the street, but the idea of driving home right now felt like giving up. I turned in the opposite direction of my car and walked down the sidewalk.

Hilliardsville was a small upscale town, with tasteful office buildings and small boutiques. I scanned the windows as I passed them, checking for help wanted signs, although I had no more experience with retail than I did with office work.

All of the optimism I'd felt earlier drained out of me, like air from a balloon. My new heels were pinching my toes, I was perspiring through my silk blouse and I wanted to cry.

The minute I thought of tears, they blurred my eyes. I turned blindly to the nearest door and pushed inside just to get out of the heat.

"I'm not hiring any models, sorry." The voice had a nasal, dismissive quality, and I wiped furiously at my eyes, my gaze darting around to find the source. The room I stood in was filled with huge canvases, each showing a different smiling face. From behind one that reached nearly to the ceiling stepped a man a little shorter than me. He had bright red hair and anxious brown eyes.

"Pardon?" I was completely at a loss.

"Isn't that why you're here? Aren't you a model?" He blinked up at me, and I thought he looked a little like an owl.

"No. No, sorry. I'm just—I was looking for a place to get out of the heat." I lifted one foot. "And my shoes hurt."

"You've been crying." He put his hands on his hips. "What's wrong, honey? Someone giving you trouble?"

"Uh—I just—I had a job interview and the guy was an asshole." I closed my eyes. "I'm sorry. I shouldn't have said that."

"Oh, sweetie, don't worry on account of me. I might look young and innocent, but these ears are hardly virgin." He winked. "And I got news for you. All men are assholes."

I shook my head. "Not all of them. Anyway, I'm sorry for bothering you." I took a quick glance around the room again. "Did you take all these pictures?"

"They're portraits, and yes, I did. I'm a photographer. I do family portraits, and on occasion, shoots for local newspapers and magazines." He stuck out one hand. "Paulie Tyrese, at your service."

"Paulie Tyrese." I tried out the words on my tongue. "That's a wonderful name."

"Thanks, I picked it out myself." He hooked a thumb at his chest. "Born plain old Paul Dubbersmith. But I wanted something more glamorous for the biz. Don't you think Tyrese sounds exotic?"

"It really does." I nodded. "And your work is great. I like taking pictures, too, but I just have an old Minolta. I always wanted something better. Remember the pictures of Jackie Kennedy, back when she was the Inquiring Photographer? I thought that looked like fun."

"Oh, Jackie." Paulie closed his eyes and lifted his clasped hands to his mouth, as though he were praying. "What a lady, huh? And a decent photog, too." He opened one eye and studied me. As though his stare was just as intense, somehow it didn't unnerve me the way Dr. Newton's had. "What sort of job were you applying for?"

He jumped from topic to topic so quickly, I frowned, trying to keep up. "Oh, receptionist. But I probably wouldn't have gotten it in any event, not if the jerk hadn't been interested in me for more than— well, how I look. I don't have experience and that seems like the key. I guess it's back to the drawing board for me."

Paulie frowned, his lips drawing together until they pursed. "What can you do?"

I shrugged. "I don't know. Anything I put my mind to, I'd say. I graduated from college, and I was a wife for two years." I paused. "I'm divorced."

The man's forehead wrinkled. "So?"

"Some people find that to be a problem."

He laughed. "I'm the last one to cast stones, believe me. But I'll tell you what. I could use someone around here to help me keep things on schedule and running. And by things, I mean me. I get into the dark room and I lose track of time. Could you do that?"

A spark of hope tindered in my chest. "I'm sure I could."

"And maybe come with me on some of the location shoots, too. They're all local, so it would be around town, or maybe just a half-hour away. Would that work?"

"Of course. I don't have anything else going on in my life. I'd be able to work around the clock if you needed me."

"Honey, never tell anyone that. They'll take you up on it. But good to know you have some flexibility. Now I can't pay too much, but I promise, I'll be fair."

I shook my head. "I don't need to make a fortune. Just enough to supplement my—" I dropped my voice. "My alimony."

"Sweetheart, if you've got alimony coming in, don't you say it like it's a dirty word. I'm thinking you earned every cent. Can you start tomorrow?"

"Sure." I nodded. "What time do you want me here?"

"We start at ten, so maybe around nine-thirty so I can show you the ropes. There aren't many of them, don't worry. It's going to be mostly learn-on-the-job and just be ready to do what I ask."

I grinned. "Sounds kind of like being married."

Paulie laughed. "You're not wrong, honey, but trust me, I'm not looking for that. You'll never have to worry about this boss getting fresh with you, so put your pretty head at ease."

August 7, 1965
Dear Tom,
I wasn't going to write again so soon when I haven't heard anything from you in a few days, but I had to tell you—guess what? I got a job!

It wasn't with the dental office my brother-in-law had arranged, because that dentist is a dirty bird. He tried to cop a feel in his office during the interview, but somehow I got up the nerve to knee him in the—well, what you taught me is called the balls. And I got out of there fast. I ended up ducking into this little shop and met a man named Paulie Tyrese. He's a photographer, and he hired me to be his receptionist/schedule minder/at-work wife. Now don't worry—Paulie's not looking at me that way. I like him a lot, but he's an odd little man.

The other day, we had an engaged couple come in to have their picture done for the newspaper. After they left, I said to Paulie, "Well, she was very pretty, wasn't she?" I expected him to have something to say, because really, the girl was "built" as my ex and his friends used to say.

But Paulie just said, "I didn't notice her, but the guy—geez-o-Pete! Did you see those arms? Even through his shirt you could make out the muscles!"

I thought that was a little odd.

But no matter, Paulie is wonderful to me and we have the best time. I've reorganized his scheduling, and I answer the phone while he's working. I went on one location shoot with him, out to a pretty garden where one of the local boutiques was doing a fashion shoot for their fall advertisements. One of the men setting it up saw me and said I should be modeling, too, instead of being behind the scenes, and Paulie said, "Leave her alone! She's too damn smart to be a model. Shame on you for only seeing a pretty face."

That made me feel good, that someone appreciates me for more than how I look.

Everything else is good. I'm enclosing some pictures of my apartment now that it's all done, so you can see my new digs. I'd love it if you could send me some of you, too, and where you are, if you can.

Until then, I'm still—
Caroline
Your Something

Chapter Five

August 15, 1965
Dear Caroline,
Congratulations, baby! I just got the letter about your new job. That's great. Do you still like it? Sounds like it's right up your alley, and this Paulie is a smart guy to see what a gem he has in you. I was laughing as you described him—so do you think he's gay?

But I wasn't laughing when you wrote about the dentist. Damn, Caroline, I want to get the first plane out of here and go beat the living shit out of that asshole. What the hell was he thinking? I hope you told your brother-in-law why you didn't get the job. Guys like that prick make me mad.

I'm glad, though, that you kicked him in the balls. Good for you—that's my girl! You stood up for yourself.

Everything here's good. Well, as good as it can be, anyway. Those new divisions of MPs moved in, so we don't have to run all over the country anymore. It's been hotter than hell here, but that sure isn't new. There was another café bombing, and one of our guys was hurt pretty bad. The worst part is the not knowing. If I could wake up in the morning and know—okay, today I'm going into battle. Then I think I could deal with it. But I go along my day, thinking it's routine, and then a goddam building explodes in front of me. So then every day feels like it could be a bad one, until we get enough boring routine days in a row, and I get lulled into relaxing again.

Sorry. I didn't mean to bring you down. But sometimes it feels like maybe what we're doing here doesn't matter, and I'm wasting precious days and weeks of my life. When you see the death and destruction, you start to realize that we don't have all the time in the world. And baby, one thing I'm realizing more and more is that if my days are numbered, I want to spend as many of them with you as I can.

On a happier note, I did manage to get some pictures for you. Some are just the landscape around here, a few are the city and then I got a buddy to take one of Benny and me, and one of just me. Sorry about that. I'm kind of scared to send it to you, because maybe I'm not as good-looking as you remember. Just remember, even if I'm not the prettiest guy, I got the moves, baby.

I was thinking about what you said a few letters back, about not knowing how to touch yourself. How to get yourself off. You should be doing that, if you're not going to find a guy to do it for you. Until I can come back and do it for you daily. Hourly? If I could, baby, if I could . . .

There's no wrong way to do it, and it's not something to be ashamed about. But I thought maybe I could help you. If you had something to read, and some instructions—you know, just until you get the hang of it.

Are you lying in bed? I can just picture you, your head on the pillow and your hair spread out all over. That night in Ocean City, your hair smelled like sunshine and the sea. I wish I could capture that scent.

Hold this letter in your left hand for now. Use your other hand to just brush over your nipples. Oh, baby, those nipples. I'm getting hard thinking about them. Just skim over them for now until they get stiff, standing up straight. Think about how it felt when I sucked them into my mouth. Now pinch them a little, gently at first, and then harder if you want. Close your eyes for a minute and picture me with my head bent over your gorgeous tits. Feel my tongue pressing your nipples against the roof of my mouth.

Ahhhh, baby, you're killing me. Okay, now that you've got yourself fired up a little, slide that hand down your stomach, between your legs. I hope you're wet. I hope your fingers are slip-sliding all over those luscious folds. Get to know them a little. Just play. And then move one finger to the top, to find something that feels like a little knob. A little button. That's your clit. Press down on it—it should feel really, really good.

I'm remembering having my lips around your clit, with the tip of my tongue teasing against it. Yeah, I'm even harder. While I'm sitting here alone writing this, my hand's on my cock. I'm imagining that it's your hand, though.

Back to business. Slide one finger into the opening of your pussy. Pump it in and out a little, just to get used to it, and then add another finger. If you can do it, use your thumb to press against your clit while you're doing that.

Keep moving those fingers, baby. You might have to drop this page at this point, and use your other hand on your tits again. God, I'm picturing you laying in your bed, getting yourself off, and I'm going to put down my pen for a minute.

I'm back. You know what I did? I leaned back in my chair, took out my cock—God, I was so hard, it hurt—and I thought of you with your hands between your legs, stroking that sweet, wet pussy, and I closed my eyes. I pumped my hand around my dick, thinking of your hips lifting up, arching against your own hand as you come, hard. It didn't take long before I was coming, too, spurting over my hand and stomach. It was a relief and it also made me miss you even more.

I hope that while you're reading this, you're panting, because you just came hard, too. And Dr. Tom's prescription is that you should do that at least three times a week. You got to keep that pussy in shape until I can come back and take care of it myself.

I'll write again soon, baby. Don't worry about me, and tell me how your job's coming along.

Love,
Tom

August 27, 1965
Dear Tom,
Thank you so much for sending me those pictures. I love that I can imagine where you are now. And you don't have to worry—you are just as hunky as I remembered. Matter of fact, when I saw your face again, I cried. Because I'd forgotten how handsome you are. And then at the same time, even though I'd forgotten, I also knew you'd changed since you've been over there. Your face is thinner. It's not a bad thing, but it makes me worry. Are things worse than you're telling me?

But your eyes are just as deep, and in that picture it felt like you were looking right into my soul. It felt good. But it made me miss you even more, if that's possible.

I have your picture propped up next to my bed, but I didn't put it in a frame, because (and don't laugh) I tuck it into my purse when I leave the house. I like to have it with me. The other night, though, my mother came over for dinner. My father still won't come over, and he doesn't really talk to me when I visit them. But I talked Mother into having dinner with Diana and me, doing a girls' night. She went into my bedroom to see the new bedspread I'd been telling her about, and she came out holding your picture.

So I had to come clean to both her and to my sister. I want you to know, it wasn't that I was hiding you. It was just that I loved having something that was just mine. Someone I didn't have to share. Of course, I didn't tell them EVERYTHING—just that I'd met you at the shore and that we were writing to each other. But the way Diana was eyeing me, I'm pretty sure she knows we didn't just hold hands on the beach.

I keep you next to my bed because I've been following doctor's orders. I read your letter to pieces, and I keep it under my pillow, but by now, I don't even have to read it. I just use my imagination. I pretend my fingers are yours, or I pretend your mouth is on my pussy. I slip three fingers into me and pretend it's your big cock. And I imagine my lips are sucking on you, that I can feel you in my mouth.

I wish it weren't just pretend.

My job is still going great. Paulie and I have such a good time every day. He tells me hiring me was the best decision he ever made, and that makes me feel so good. Needed.

But I have to tell you a funny story. In one of your letters, you asked me if Paulie was gay. I didn't know what you meant, but I was pretty sure it wasn't happy. I thought about it, and I was going to ask Diana, but I wasn't sure if she'd know, either. So I was at work, and it was just the two of us. Paulie was setting up some new displays, and I was updating our schedule book. I took a deep breath and said, "Paulie, do you know what it means to be gay?"

He dropped the canvas he was holding and said, "What the hell did you say?"

I told him the whole story, about you and about your letter and what you said. He just about fell over laughing, and he explained to me what it means. Well, then I almost fell over. I mean, Tom, I knew there were some boys who were a little effeminate or something, but I didn't know about—well, that!

After I got over my shock, Paulie insisted I show him your picture. He got all excited and said you were the cutest thing he'd ever seen but not to worry, because from what I told him, you weren't his type.

Now I'm going back over all the men I ever knew and wondering if they're gay, too! I had no idea.

Paulie's been letting me take some pictures now and then. He says I have a good eye for spacing and composition, and that if I keep at it, maybe eventually he could bring me on as a partner. Can you even imagine? I've loved learning how to use the camera and all the lenses, and about lighting and everything.

It's good to feel like I'm part of something. It helps me not think about what might be going on with you. I watch the evening news now. I didn't used to, except in passing when my dad had it on. Now I eat it up. And when I see soldiers, I want to go ask them if they're heading to southeast Asia. I think about bombs going off and restaurants exploding. I think about people shooting in the jungle, like I've seen on the news.

But during the day when I'm keeping my mind on photography and business, it's a little better. It's not like at night, when I miss you the most. Sometimes, while I'm trying to sleep, I imagine what our days might be like if you weren't in Vietnam. I was thinking about what you said our life would be. We'd probably be in California, right? Maybe I'd be starting law school right about now. I'd know your aunt, and your friends, and we'd be together every night.

Even though that isn't our reality, and maybe it never will be, it helps me to think of what might have been.

    Love until next time,
    Caroline
    Your Something

Chapter Six

September 19, 1965
Dear Tom,
I told you early on that I wouldn't blame you if you decided not to write me anymore. If you just didn't reply. And I wouldn't. But I'm going to add a caveat. If you change your mind, please just send me a quick note and say you're okay but you won't be writing anymore. All right? Because otherwise, I'll go crazy. Kind of like I am right now.

I haven't heard from you in a long time. No letters in almost two weeks, and I'm so worried. The men on the news look more and more serious every night, and I overhear people talking and shaking their heads.

I kept thinking—if something had happened, I'd know. But then again, I thought . . . how? I'm not your wife. I'm not listed on any next-of-kin. I don't know if you ever told your aunt about us, and I realized I don't even know her last name. You mentioned her in a letter as Aunt Cissy, but other than that first name and the fact that she's an attorney in California, I don't have any information. You could disappear off the face of the earth and I'd never know.

Tom, I hope you can tell by how I've been writing to you lately that I'm serious about you. About us. I understand if you don't, and maybe when I wrote about me telling my mother and Diana and Paulie about you, it spooked you. If so, I'm sorry.

Just please write to me. And please be okay.
Caroline

September 21, 1965
Dear Caroline,

Baby, I'm so sorry. I'm fine, and I don't have any plans to stop writing to you. Your letter just about broke my heart.

We got word right after I sent my last letter that Benny, me and a few other of our guys had been assigned to a special detail upcountry. Something had gone down and they needed us to help with the investigation. I didn't have time to write or anything to get word to you. And I didn't worry at first, because I figured we'd be there and back, but it ended up being a lot more involved.

I just got back about ten minutes ago, saw your letters and opened the latest one last—and my heart dropped to my feet. Just so you know: I told Benny as soon as we got over here, that if anything happened to me, he needed to write to you, get word to you, and go see you when he gets home. I know that sounds morbid, but it's the kind of stuff we have to think about here.

And so you know: Aunt Cissy is more generally known as Susannah Polk, and I put her address and telephone number at the bottom of this page. She knows about you. She knows your name and your address. I promise, honey. I'm not planning to go anywhere, but if the worst happened, you wouldn't be in the dark.

Now let's talk about everything else.

I just about busted a gut laughing about you asking Paulie what gay meant. I guess maybe it's something we say on the West coast, or maybe you were just brought up better than me! He sounds like a decent guy, though. I'm glad you're working for him. Tell him thanks for taking good care of my girl.

I love that you keep my picture by your bed and that you take it with you. Yours that you sent me is about worn out because I carry it everywhere in my pocket. Maybe you can get Paulie to take another one and send it to me.

And you can bet tonight, I'll have it out along with your letter, and my cock in my hand, because all these weeks out in the field meant no privacy. They were some long-ass nights, remembering you, thinking of you, and not being able to do a damn thing about it. I was afraid I was about to start having wet dreams again like when I was a teenager.

I'll write again tomorrow, I promise, and every day as long as I can to catch up. Meanwhile, have you made any new friends outside of Paulie? You haven't mentioned anyone and I don't want you to be lonely.

I guess I should tell you again that you should find a guy to date and forget about me . . . but I promised to be honest. And honesty makes me say—I don't want any man touching you but me, ever again.

Love,
Tom
November 1, 1965
Dear Tom,

I feel so spoiled. I just picked up my mail downstairs and had three more letters from you. You really did write every day this month. I feel like I've been right next to you in some of those letters, and my dreams every night have become even more vivid. If I were a man, I might even call them wet dreams (thanks again for explaining to me what those are).

I was excited to write to you today and tell you I met someone last night. Now before you get worried, she's a girl. It was Halloween and the building had a party for all the residents. I was hanging out by the punch bowl and this girl with black hair wearing a witch's hat came over. She asked me to save her—this guy wouldn't leave her alone. So we decided to stick together. We hit it off—her name is Rose, and she lives two floors down from me. She's married, but her husband's in the navy, and he's on a ship somewhere for a year. So we have some stuff in common.

Rose doesn't know anyone around here. They were stationed near Philadelphia when her husband shipped out, so she decided to just stay in the area. She's a secretary at a bank in Cherry Hill. We already made plans to have drinks together on Friday night. Drinks! Can you imagine? I've never done anything like that before in my life. It sounds so grown-up and glamorous.

How are things over there? You haven't said too much lately. That makes me wonder if they're worse. My mother told me that Mrs. Winter (she goes to our church) has a grandson over in Vietnam, and he was wounded. I think he's going to be okay, but it feels like this war is coming much closer.

I'm enclosing the new picture of me Paulie took. See what you think.

Love,
Caroline
Your Something

Chapter Seven

TELEGRAM
1965 DEC 4
CAROLINE: TOM SLIGHTLY INJURED IN HOTEL BLAST. COMPLETE RECOVERY EXPECTED. MORE INFORMATION VIA LETTER FOLLOWS. BEST, BEN DILLIARD

December 5, 1965
Dear Caroline,
Please don't be upset, Tom is fine. He asked me to write to you for him because his right hand is still bandaged. But he is going to recover just fine, and he wanted you to know that.

Now I'm also going to tell you what he wouldn't. Your man is a hero. He got hurt in the initial blast, and then he carried ten men to safety before the medics finally forced him to stop and let them care for him.

It was scary as all hell, and a goddam mess, but we're both okay.

Tom says I need to stop blabbering nonsense and tell you he'll write as soon as he can use his hand. So I guess I will, and I'll close by saying you got a fine man here, and I look forward to a day when him and me can both be back stateside. Maybe some time you two and my wife and me can all meet up together, and then we'll laugh about all this mess.
Best,
Ben Dilliard

December 5, 1965
Dear Tom,
Oh, my God, what happened? Are you really going to be all right? I saw something in the paper about the hotel explosion in Saigon and then they said there were American soldiers living there, and I thought—well, that can't be the same place Tom is. Right then, my buzzer sounded and the doorman called up that I had a telegram.

Tom, I have never fainted in all my life, but at that moment, I thought I was going to. My hands were shaking and my heart was pounding. I managed to get to the door and met the delivery man, and then I was ripping it open and the first words I saw were "complete recovery expected". And then I could breathe again.

Please write me as soon as you can. Until then, I'm going to keep believing you're okay. And I'll keep writing, so you can read the letters even if you can't write back yet.
Love,
Caroline
Your Something

December 14, 1965
Dear Caroline,
Hey, baby, it's me! Finally. The old hand is back in commission, not completely better yet, but good enough to write. I couldn't wait any longer.

I'm so sorry again, honey. The first thought I had, once the adrenaline wore off, was that I had to tell you I was all right. I made Benny go right away to telegram you, and then I made him write to you the next day. I was glad when I got your letter that you'd gotten both of those.

It was pretty crazy. We were sleeping, and I was dreaming about you. In my dream, you were here with me, and I was holding you in my arms. And then someone was shooting at us, and I was trying to protect you. I woke up slowly, realizing the shots I heard weren't just in my dream. I jumped out of bed and looked out the window, and I saw the flash of guns, but I couldn't tell where they were. I yelled for Benny to wake up, and next thing I knew, the whole damn room was shaking and the explosion was so loud.

I got knocked down and a piece of something hit my neck. I jumped up, though, and we headed right away to where the worst of the damage was. That's where my hand got hurt, pulling rubble off some of the men.

Anyway, like Benny said, it was crazy and surreal and a goddam mess, but we're all okay.

Here's the good news, baby. Partly because of timing and partly because of what happened, I got approved for some R and R in Hawaii in early January. I'll have seven days there.

Caroline, I know this is a lot to ask, but God, I can't help asking it anyway. Will you meet me in Hawaii?

If you think you might, I'll telegram you as soon as I have the definite date. You'd have to be ready to go at a moment's notice.

I understand if you feel like this is asking too much or if it's not right. Under normal circumstances, I wouldn't think of asking you to do this, but baby, if I can see you—it would mean the world.

I'll be waiting for your answer.
Love,

Tom

December 22, 1965
Dear Tom,
YES!! Yes, yes, yes, yes, yes.
I will fly to Hawaii. I'll be waiting for your telegram.
Yes, yes, yes.
Love,
Caroline

TELEGRAM
1966 JANUARY 4
WILL ARRIVE OAHU 1/7. MEET AT FT. DERUSSY. COUNTING DAYS. TOM

Chapter Eight

The waiting room at Fort DeRussy wasn't crowded, and few of the women sitting in the hard plastic chairs were talking to each other. All of us kept our eyes on the window, where we'd been told that the buses from the airport would arrive.

I'd landed at the same airport about five hours before. All I'd seen of Hawaii so far had been through the windows of the airplane as we landed and the taxi that drove me here, where I'd been waiting.

I'd been alone in the room when I arrived; from what I'd overheard, most of the other women had arrived the day before and already had hotel rooms. I'd eyed up the beautiful hotels as we drove past, wishing for a comfortable bed after my fifteen-hour flight, but I had no idea what Tom had planned. He'd only given me the vaguest information, mostly, I assumed, because he didn't know much himself.

The majority of the women in the room with me wore wedding rings. A few were much older, and I wondered if some might be mothers here to see their sons. Most of us, though, were all around the same age. Four or five were obviously pregnant. But for all of our differences, we all wore the same expression, a mixture of anxiety and anticipation.

A squeal of brakes jerked my attention back to the outside, where a brown bus was coming to a halt. My heart pounded in my chest; it had been nearly seven months since I'd seen Tom, and even then, it had only been for one night. We'd known each other for about twelve hours. Yes, our letters over the past months had been honest and intimate, but the idea of being in the same room with him again . . . I couldn't wait, but at the same time, I was terrified.

The doors of the bus opened, and suddenly everyone in the waiting room was on her feet. Most of them surged toward the window, but I hung back, shy.

Men poured out of the bus, and I heard one woman cry out. As the soldiers came in, each one paused in the doorway, searching the waiting faces with unashamed eagerness. I watched, feeling a little like a voyeur, as couples found each other and embraced. I almost wanted to cry, seeing the depth of emotion.

I watched the doorway, my eyes seeking Tom. For a dizzying moment, I forgot what he looked like. What if we didn't recognize each other? What if things between us were awkward? What if he didn't like me anymore, once he saw me again? What if I—

"Caroline."

I hadn't heard his voice in over half a year, and yet it was as familiar to me as if I'd spoken to him every day. Shivers ran down my spine as I turned and looked up at him.

His face was definitely thinner, as I'd noticed in the pictures. But his eyes were just as vivid blue, and the longing in them was the same, too. He lifted one finger to touch my cheek, and to my everlasting mortification, I burst into tears.

"Baby." Tom pulled me against him, pressing my face into his chest. I sucked in a deep breath, absorbing his scent, and leaned into him.

"I'm sorry." I sniffled against him. "I just—I think part of me wasn't sure I'd ever see you again. I'm just so happy to see you. To be with you." I drew back and framed his face with my hand, all at once eager to touch as much of him as I could. My fingers trailed to his neck, skimming the still-visible scar. "Does it hurt?"

He caught my hand and brought it to his lips, turning it over so that he could kiss the palm. "Not much."

"And your hand?" I lifted it up.

"Good as new." He bent to murmur in my ear. "Ready for action."

A burning need rose within me. "I'm really happy to hear that."

"Ladies and gentlemen, we need you to move into the orientation room now, so that we can let you all get started on your week of R and R." A uniformed man spoke from the doorway. "Let's get this over with."

Tom grimaced. "We have to go in and listen to the instructions, and then we can get out of here." He lowered his hand to my back and guided me along with the crowd.

"I didn't find a hotel or anything yet." I craned my head back to look at him. "I only got here this morning. Or this afternoon. Honestly, I don't know what time of day it is."

He laughed. "Me neither. Don't worry, we'll grab a taxi and find a hotel as soon as we get through the typical Army bullshit."

~~~

Thanks to the advice we were given during the orientation, Tom and I were able to rent a car and find a hotel in record time. I waited in the car while he checked us in; even though neither of us knew a soul on this island, it didn't feel right to flout our unmarried but shacking up status.

Tom carried in his duffel and both of my suitcases, while I trailed behind him, admiring the way his khaki trousers fitted his backside. I'd expected to be more nervous about the idea of being alone in a hotel room with him, but apparently my body hadn't gotten that message, since I was already incredibly turned on.

And I wasn't the only one. The minute the door closed behind me, Tom dropped the bags and took two long steps toward me. He held my face in his hands for one moment, staring down at me.

"Do you know how long I've been wanting to do this?" Without waiting for me to answer, he took my lips, consuming them, consuming me, and swallowing the moan wrenched from my throat. His mouth was hot, and his tongue stroked against me, searching and tasting and teasing. I met it with my own, reacquainting myself with his texture.

My arms rose of their own accord to wrap around his neck, my fingers smoothing the bristles of his hair. When Tom broke the kiss to catch his breath, I ran my lips over his jaw and down his neck. "God, Tom. I can't believe I'm really here with you. I keep thinking I'm going to wake up and realize it's a dream."

"Maybe I need to do something to let you know it's real." He slid his hands up my back, searching for the tab of my dress zipper. He lowered it slowly, touching the warm skin beneath the material and leaning away from me just enough to let the top of the dress drop between us. "Baby. Oh my God, these tits. I've been dreaming of them, but they're better than I remembered." He brought his mouth to where my breasts swelled over the edge of the bra.

"I think when you touch me, I'm going to go up in flames." I arched my back, thrusting my boobs against his face. "I just want your hands on me. And your mouth. And just you."

"We can make that happen." Tom tugged down one cup of my bra, the tops of his fingers brushing my nipple. I moaned, loudly, and he laughed.

"I guess I don't have to teach you to use your words anymore, huh?"

I guided his mouth toward my boob. "I'd say I'm doing okay telling you what I want. And right now, I want you to suck my tits. Touch my nipples." I raked my fingernails over his crewcut. "I've been practicing. Imagining how I'd say it."

"I like your kind of warm-up, baby." His lips closed around the stiff rosy peak, and I gasped, clutching at the back of his head to hold him to me.

"So . . . so good." I breathed out the words as he shifted his mouth to the other side.

"You have no idea." Tom's voice vibrated against me, and I shivered in pleasure. "When I was in the worst places, or felt like I was never going to get out of there, I just thought about you. You've been my touchstone over these months."

My fingers found the buttons on the front of his shirt, and I began undoing them. "I need to touch you. I want to make sure every bit of you is okay."

"You don't trust me?" Tom nudged my chin up with his fingers. "You don't think I'd tell you if I were hurt?"

I lifted one eyebrow. "Honey, I'm telling you I need to examine every single inch of your body. Close up. Are you going to complain?"

A broad smile spread over his face. "Not one bit. I'm all yours."

Tugging his shirt from his pants, I breathed out in appreciation. "I'd forgotten how gorgeous your chest is." The flat brown discs of his nipples were right at my eye level, so I took advantage of that to lick a circle around one, smiling when he rewarded me with a groan. "This part seems functional still." I pushed his shirt the rest of the way from his shoulders and stepped closer, fitting my body against his. The ridge beneath the fly of his pants made me grin, and I ground into him just a little bit. "And from what I feel, other parts are also rising to the occasion."

"But you should probably check it out to make absolutely sure, right?" Tom began to undo his pants.

"Of course. Being thorough is . . ." My voice trailed off as his trousers fell to floor, leaving him in his boxers, his cock jutting out, yearning toward me. "Uh, my duty." Pointing to the bed, I added, "You lay down to make my job easier."

"Baby, I'm nothing if not easy." He sat down on the edge of the mattress and then swung his legs over, stretching out. "God, this feels good. A real bed, with real, soft sheets and a decent pillow."

I shrugged my dress the rest of the way off my body and stood before him in just my bra, panties, garter belt and stockings and heels. Tom's mouth fell open a little bit, and his eyes dilated. Reaching back, I began to pull pins from my hair and let it fall around me.

"But best of all, a real woman." He held out one hand. "C'mere, baby. If I can't touch you in the next second, I'm going to die right here."

I climbed onto the bed, kicking off my shoes as I went. "We can't have that. That'd be ironic, wouldn't it—you make it through seven months of war and die of desire on R and R?"

"So get over here and make sure it doesn't happen. God, baby. I don't know what I want to do first. I want to be inside you now, but I want to make you wild first. I want to taste every inch of you."

"We have time." I knelt beside him and bent to brush kisses along his cheek, to his ear. "More than twelve hours this time. For now, just lay here and let me . . . finish my examination."

"I'd never stand in the way of that." Tom threaded his fingers through my hair. "Have at me."

"Wise man." I straddled his body. "Let's see. I know your nipples are still good, so maybe it's time to move . . . lower." As I spoke, I lowered my mouth to his ribs, tasting each one and then walking my lips and tongue over his flat stomach, following the line of light brown hair that led me to the waistband of his boxers. My heart began to beat erratically. With slowness that was both teasing and excruciating, I untied the waistband and eased it lower.

Tom's cock stood tall, long and thick. I wrapped one hand around him, moving it up and down slowly.

"Oh, God. Caroline. Baby. I never thought I'd get to . . . your hands on me. So fucking good."

"Is it just my hands you like?" I lay so that my head rested on his stomach. "Is that all?"

His body shook, but I wasn't sure if it was from laughter or sobs. "I think I told you last summer . . . as long as it's you, as long as you're touching me, anything you do is right."

"Hmmm. Then maybe . . ." I lifted my head and brought my mouth to his erection. "Maybe this would work." I licked just the head of his cock, pausing when his breath hissed and his hips jerked. "Too much?"

"No . . . just wait one minute. I need to think of something else or I'm going to shoot my load all over you before I can even . . ." His face screwed up in concentration for a minute and then relaxed. "Okay. I'm all right for a few more minutes. Proceed."

"Thanks." I didn't hesitate this time to take all of him into my mouth, giddiness singing through my blood at the feel of his huge dick hitting the back of my throat. I sucked at him, slowly and surely working my mouth up and down his length, one hand holding the base and the other cupping his balls. His hands fisted into the comforter at his sides, and I knew he was struggling to hold onto control. I slowed a little, releasing him with one final kiss to the flared head.

"Caroline, in the pocket of my pants—there's a condom. Can you get it?"

I frowned a little—I'd wanted him with no barriers between us—but now wasn't the time to argue. I leaned off the bed to snag his pants, fumbled in the pocket and fished out the flat square. "Got it."

"Put it on me?" He folded his hands behind his head and watched me with heavy-lidded eyes.

"Mmmmhmmm." I ripped the packet carefully, trying to remember how I'd done it last year. Centering it over his rigid cock, I rolled the rubber down. "But you know, I was thinking. You've been such a good teacher. Maybe first . . . before we move on . . . you'd like to see how well I've learned."

"Baby, I can already tell what a fast learner you are. But definitely, show me."

I lifted my knee over his legs again, positioning myself so that I sat just below his dick. "Well . . . let's start here." I reached behind my back and unhooked my bra, freeing my boobs. I brought my fingers to my own nipples and circled them until they stiffened, then I cupped both breasts, lifting them together. "I know you love my tits. It feels so good when I touch myself here and imagine it's your mouth on me."

His mouth was open and his breath came in short pants, but he didn't speak.

Trailing my hands down my body, I slipped two fingers between my legs. "And thanks to you, I know that when I'm wet . . . like this. . ." I lifted up two fingers, glistening with my own essence. "It's a good thing. It means I'm so turned on, I could come if you even breathed on me." I returned my hand to my pussy, rubbing slowly against my slippery folds.

"That's it. I can't stand it." With a groan that sounded more like a roar, Tom rolled, pinning me beneath him. "Can't take another minute, baby. Need to have my mouth on you."

He put his words into action right away, tearing off my panties and spreading my legs. With a strangled gasp, he lowered his mouth onto my core. There was nothing slow about the way his lips fastened onto my clit and sucked. And when his tongue speared into me, pleasure that had been building to a simmer exploded into unspeakable bliss, sending me spiraling even as I held his head against me, my hips canting and jerking.

Words that I never used spilled from my mouth. "Tom, baby, God, fuck, so good, don't stop, oh, honey I'm coming so hard against your beautiful mouth, suck me, baby. Oh, so good."

He kept licking and stroking until I'd settled a little, and then he kissed his way up, stopping at my boobs to push them together and sucking a rose-colored tip into his mouth. I moaned, and he glanced up at me.

"Again, baby. You're going to come again. I'm going to make you come again, and then I'm going to be inside you, and you're going to come again around my cock . . ."

His words were enough to bring me to the edge again, but when he added his fingers between my legs, rubbing relentlessly against my too-sensitive clit, I was crying out again. Tom growled against my nipple and held himself over me, lining up his erection to my entrance.

"Are you ready, baby? Ready for me? I'm about to die, Caroline. I want you so bad. All I want is you. No one else, no one else ever . . ."

"Yes." I ground out the single syllable. "Yes, come inside me now. Please, please, please . . ."

On my last plea, Tom plunged inside me, seating himself so deep that I wanted to sing in joy. He stayed there for a beat, and I was certain that time had stopped, standing still for us as we were joined once again. I didn't want it to start flowing again. Here was where I wanted to stay, forever.

And then he began to move, slowly stroking out and in, and I was perfectly fine with time marching on, because each thrust was sweeter than the one before.

"Caroline, baby. Oh, God. You feel so good. All I've wanted since that morning was to be back inside you. Honey, I can't . . . oh God. Fuck, fuck, *fuck.*"

With one last drive, his body tensed into one long hard muscle, his jaw clenched and eyes closed. The pulsing of his dick inside me hit that one sweet spot that made me lift up to meet him again, colors exploding behind my eyes.

We fell back onto the pillows, neither of us able to talk for several moments. Tom rolled off me, collapsing onto his back, and I curled against him, resting my head on his chest where my ear pressed into the reassuring beat of his heart.

"Caroline." Tom's hand smoothed over my hair. "Caroline, I missed you so much. God, you don't know." He sighed and then lifted his head to kiss my forehead. "C'mere, honey. I need to kiss you."

I shimmied up a little. "I'm not sure how much I can move at the moment. But for a kiss . . ." I covered his lips with mine. "I can always make the effort for a kiss from you."

"Caroline." He held my face between his two hands, his eyes searching mine. "I love you. I promised myself I wouldn't say that to you until I was back stateside for good, but I can't help it. I love you, baby. I want you, now and for always."

My lips curled into a smile, even as tears threatened. "So I can call myself your girlfriend now? I mean, not that being your something hasn't been just fine, but . . ."

"Honey, you're more than my something. You're my everything. And I don't care what you call yourself, as long as I can call you mine."

I raised myself up on my elbows, looking down into the face I'd fallen for the minute I'd seen it. "Baby, I'm yours. I always have been, and I always will be."

Through the open window of the hotel room, plumeria-scented air teased over our entwined bodies. Tom wrapped his arms around me again, and as I tucked my head beneath his chin, I knew I never wanted to leave this time or place.

Paradise was mine, as long as I was his.

Caroline and Tom's story continues in
Save It For Me
Good Vibrations Book #3
Releasing June, 2016

Read the beginning of Tom and Caroline's story in
More Than Words
Good Vibrations Book #1

Baby, I'm Yours
Play List

Back in My Arms Again--The Supremes
Go Now--The Magnificent Moodies
Bye, Bye Baby--The Four Seasons
Baby, I'm Yours--Barbara Lewis
Turn, Turn, Turn!--The Byrds
Unchained Melody--The Righteous Brothers
I'll Never Find Another You--The Seekers
We Gotta Get Out of This Place--The Animals
You Were On My Mind--We Five

A Note from Emma

When authors talk about research in relation to an erotic romance novel, most of the time they're talking about something . . . fun. Hot. Sexy.

But the research for this short was much more serious and sobering. Although this is fiction, it was important to me to get the facts right.

Just about everything in this story that relates to Vietnam is accurate. A Military Police division did deploy to Vietnam from Fort Dix in 1965, though the timing was tweaked slightly for the purposes of this story. The 716th Military Police Battalion has a long and brave history, and I encourage you to read more about these courageous men.

The bombing of the barracks is also factual. The Metropole Hotel in Saigon was the target of a truck bomb on December 4, 1965, with the results very much as described here.

R&R in Hawaii for soldiers fighting in Vietnam didn't actually commence until 1966, but as that is part of my personal history and integral to the story, I stretched time a little to make it work. Everything as related to R&R is accurate.

Caroline and Tom's story will continue for several more books. I hope you'll continue on this journey with them.

Thank you, as always, for reading.

About Emma

Emma Fallon is a southern girl with a penchant for long nights under the stars with hot men. She writes and reads erotic romance and has a special weakness for historical erotica. She can be enticed to do just about anything. . .as long as there's chocolate involved.

Follow her on Facebook! And on Twitter. . . Keep up with her on her website. . . . . .and finally, subscribe to her special events newsletter for the chance to win prizes and get sneak previews of books!

More from Emma

The Small Town Swingers Serial

Welcome to Paradise
The Heat Is On
Night Moves
Fading Into You

Good Vibrations Series

More Than Words
Baby, I'm Yours
Save It For Me

www.ingramcontent.com/pod-product-compliance
Lightning Source LLC
LaVergne TN
LVHW030242250326
834688LV00047B/1769